Nobody Asked *Me*
If I Wanted a Baby Sister

STORY AND PICTURES BY
Martha Alexander

Dial Books for Young Readers
New York

For Christina
and Leslie
and for Herry O.T.

"Oh, Mrs. Applebaum, what a beautiful baby!"
"How chubby she is!"
"What pretty blue eyes she has!"

"Hi, Amy, Alice, and Phyllis! Would your
mother like to have a beautiful baby?"

"Sure, if it's a boy."

"Mister, would you like a beautiful chubby
  baby?"

"Well, sonny, maybe we could use her in our act. Can she balance a ball?"

"Say, folks, would you like this beautiful, chubby blue-eyed baby? That basket would be perfect for her to ride in."

"I never thought of that. But we're going
to have our own baby soon! Thanks anyway!"

"I give up. Nobody wants you."

"Hi, Toby, do you know anybody who wants
a baby that nobody wants?"

"Sure, my mom. She loves babies."

"Look what we brought you, Mom!"
"Oh, what a nice baby!

What's the matter, baby? Are you hungry?

Not hungry? Is a pin sticking you?

No pins are sticking her. Maybe she just
doesn't like me. You take her, Jane.''

"This baby's impossible!
Ouch! She's pulling my hair!"

"What a loud-mouth baby!"

"Be quiet, loud-mouth baby!"

"Why, Oliver, it's *you* she wants!"

"You know, Bonnie, you're a lot smarter than I thought. Let's go tell Mom."

When you get big enough maybe we could
play horse and wagon."